Not now,
Nathan!

Also in the Definitely Daisy series:

You're a disgrace, Daisy!
Just you wait, Winona!
You must be joking, Jimmy!
I'd like a little word, Leonie!
What's the matter, Maya?

Not now, Nathan!

Jenny Oldfield

Illustrated by
Lauren Child

**Hodder
Children's
Books**

a division of Hodder Headline Limited

To Sue
(bo-bop-bop, be-bop!)

First published in Great Britain in 2001
by Hodder Children's Books

ISBN 0 340 78502 0

Printed and bound in Great Britain

Hodder Children's Books
a division of Hodder Headline Ltd
338 Euston Road
London NW1 3BH

One

'Daisy Morelli, if you can't be sensible with a triangle, I'll have to put you on yoghurt pots for the rest of the term!'

Miss Ambler's voice rose above the crash of drums and the clash of cymbals. The teacher's music lesson had run into trouble.

'Daisy, do you hear me?' Rambler Ambler shrieked.

Daisy ignored her and went on tinkling

her triangle.

At the back of the hall, Jimmy Black bashed the big drum. Maya blew into her recorder and produced a wild squeak.

'Put that triangle down!' Miss Ambler screeched. 'Daisy, do as I say!' She pushed past Winona on keyboard and Nathan on violin, making a bee-line for Daisy.

…Tinkle – tring – tinkle! Inside her head, Daisy was playing music with her favourite girl band. It was a huge gig, the stage lights were hot and blinding. Fans roared out the words to the band's number one single…

Then, *Whoosh!* The triangle vanished from Daisy's hands.

She blinked hard and looked up at Miss Ambler's angry face.

The teacher dangled the triangle in front of her. 'As I've already told you, if you can't be trusted with a proper instrument you must

join the little ones on yoghurt pots. And don't look at me like that, Daisy. It's your own fault for not listening in the first place.'

Daisy sulked and sighed. She didn't want to be on yoghurt pots with Year 2. Everyone would laugh.

From behind her precious keyboard, Winona-Stupid-Jones was already smirking and whispering about Daisy to Nathan Moss.

'Here!' Miss Ambler thrust an empty plastic pot and a wooden stick at Daisy. 'Go and sit beside Jimmy. Play only when he plays. At all other times remain silent. Got it?'

Daisy sniffed. She clambered over chairs and instruments to reach Jimmy and his giant drum.

Miss Ambler picked up her conducting stick and tapped it on the table. 'Silence!'

Squeak! Maya frowned, looked down at her recorder and shook it.

Boooom! Jimmy's hand slipped and he thumped the drum. 'Oops!' he grinned.

Bop! Daisy copied Jimmy and rapped the

base of her yoghurt pot. 'Oops!' she echoed.

'Silence!' Ambler pleaded.

Eeee-eeek! Nathan tuned his violin.

Plink-plonk! Leonie Flowers tightened the strings of her guitar.

'Please!' the teacher whined. 'We're running short of time. We only have three more days before we perform this piece in public. We must concentrate and try to get at least the opening number right!'

Squeak! Eek! Plink-plonk! Boom! Bop! … Bo-bop-bop, be-bop, be-bop, bop-bop-bop! Daisy got into a rhythm. She was the drummer for Snake Eye, the world's top girl band. Bop-di-bop, rattle-rattle-roll!

All those years of selling doughnuts from behind a stall in Marshway Shopping Centre had finally paid off.

Daisy had slaved all day over a hot doughnut stove and in the evenings she'd practised her drumming in her bedroom above the Pizza Palazzo. Bo-bop-bop, bop-bop!

Until at last her amazing talent had been spotted. One day Snake Eye had been eating Pizza in Daisy's dad's restaurant.

They'd heard the genius on the drums through the open bedroom window. They'd gone upstairs and begged her on bended knees to join the band...

'Daisy!' Miss Boring-Snoring rapped her stick on the table until it snapped in two. 'Will someone please ask Daisy Morelli to stop playing her yoghurt pot and let Winona perform her keyboard solo in peace?'

'Psst!' Jimmy broke into Daisy's daydream. 'Watch out, Ambler's about to lose it!'

Bop... bop...bo! Daisy slowed, then stopped.

'Thank you, Jimmy!' the teacher sighed. Raising her broken stick to begin conducting, she turned to Mizz Perfect.

Winona's neat little hands were poised over the shiny white keys. Her golden curls hung forward over her pink cheeks. She looked up at Miss Ambler, who waved her stick.

And Winona played.

She played like an angel, note-perfect. Her hands flew across the keyboard, her fingers hardly seeming to touch the keys.

She played on. And on.

Daisy yawned and stared out of the window at the school caretaker, Bernie King, and his dog. They were crossing the empty playground towards the soccer pitch. Bernie carried a pot of white paint and a brush. He reached the field and kneeled down to begin freshening up the white lines which marked out the pitch.

I could be out there now, this minute! Daisy sighed. *Me and Jimmy could be passing the ball, tackling, scoring goals...*

'Lovely, Winona!' Miss Ambler praised her star pupil. 'I'm sure the mums and dads who come to watch the concert on Thursday evening will love your solo!'

Yeah, yeah, yeah! Daisy muttered under
her breath. The trouble was, she knew it
was true.

'Why can't you be more like Winona?'
Daisy's mum, Angie, would sigh after she'd
watched the concert. 'She's always so neat
and tidy and so well-behaved.'

And so yuck-making! Daisy watched
Winona now, as she sat down after her
perfect solo. Winona wore a faint smile
above her crisp white collar and striped tie.
The smile said, 'Beat that!' to anyone who
dared to follow.

'Now Nathan!' Miss Ambler announced.

Nathan glanced up over the rim of his
glasses. He twitched his freckled nose, then
shooed his pet spider, Legs, from the palm of
his hand on to the sheet-music spread out
on the stand in front of him.

Daisy watched Legs take a stroll along the
black blobs that made up Nathan's music.
The spider was fat, round and black like the

notes, but three times as big. And he had long, furry legs that scuttled him across the page.

'Ugh!' Jade leaned across from the recorder section to hiss in Daisy's ear. 'That is so NOT nice!'

'Hmm.' In fact, though Daisy didn't like Nathan much, she didn't mind Legs. She was even rather fond of the unusual furry pet.

Legs lived in a big jam-jar and went everywhere with Nathan.

Nathan could let him out and Legs would sit on his desk in the sun. He would hop over the edge and dangle on a thread so fine you couldn't even see it. Then he would scramble back up in the flash of an eye.

'Nathan, which piece of violin music have you chosen to play for us on Thursday?' Miss Ambler asked sweetly.

'Please Miss, I'd like to play Strauss,' Nathan replied.

Yawn – yawn – yawnsville! Daisy opened

her mouth wide as Nathan raised his violin and tucked it under his chin.

Screech-scrape-screech! The bow scraped over the strings.

Please let this lesson finish! Daisy prayed. If this was Strauss, give her the Top Ten on Radio One every time. *Let it be lunchtime! Let me never have to play another yoghurt pot in my whole life!*

Gazing out of the window, she saw Bernie King glance at his watch and put the lid on his paint tin. Then he strode back towards the school with Fat Lennox waddling after him.

Nathan played his violin.

Zzz-zzzzz! The rest of the class fell half-asleep while Miss Ambler waved her stick and drifted into a world of her own. Daisy shuffled on her chair. She let the yoghurt pot roll from her knee on to the floor, where it landed with a small rattle and rolled away under Jimmy's drum.

Miss Ambler tutted but Nathan kept playing.

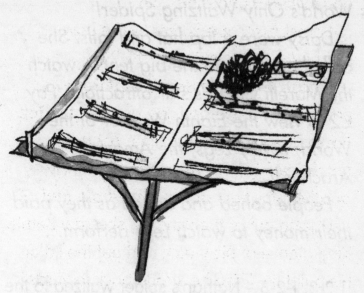

And Legs did a sort of strange dance. Daisy watched him lift his eight furry legs in time to the music, darting in-between the printed notes and down the page until he came to the edge. Then he turned and waltzed back to the top. He turned again and slid off sideways. Another swirling spin and he faced up the page. 1-2-3, 1-2-3 – the spider whirled.

* * *

...'Roll up, roll up! Come in and see the World's Only Waltzing Spider!'

Daisy wore a top hat and tails. She called people into the big tent to watch the Morelli Circus's star attraction. 'Pay £2 to view the Eighth Wonder of the World; Lovely Legs, the Amazing Arachnid!'

People oohed and aahed as they paid their money to watch Legs perform...

1-2-3, 1-2-3 – Nathan's spider waltzed to the edge of the page and disappeared on a silken thread.

'Beautiful!' Miss Ambler praised Nathan as he came to the end of his piece.

Daisy could see that the teacher was beginning to hope that Thursday might not turn out to be a total disaster after all. Tickets had been sent out to parents. Two hundred people were expected to turn up. Things had to be right.

'We have time for one more run through of

the opening number!' Miss Ambler told the class.

Daisy, Jimmy, Leonie, Jared and the rest let out a groan.

'Get ready for a racket!' Jimmy whispered to Daisy.

Miss Ambler raised her stick. 'And one, and two, and three!'

Eee-eeak! Crash! Bang! Wallop! Bop-de-bop-bop!

Outside in the playground, Bernie King glared into the hall. Fat Lennox sat down, opened his slobbering jaws and howled.

Mrs Waymann, showing visitors around the school, reached the entrance hall, heard the row and hurried them along.

Inside her office, Mrs Hannam the school secretary reached for her foam earplugs and jammed them quickly into her ears.

'Right, that's it!' Bernie burst into the hall and brought the rehearsal to an end. 'Time to clear away!'

'Couldn't you just give us two more

minutes?' Rambler Ambler pleaded.

But the caretaker shook his head. 'Sorry.
No can do. It's ten minutes to twelve, dead
on. I have to clear the hall to let the dinner
ladies set up tables. They'd have my hide
if I let you stay even two seconds over
time!'

Phew! Daisy let out a sigh of relief and
joined the scramble to leave the hall.

Jade and Maya slammed their recorders
down on the front table and scooted off.
Jimmy grappled with his drum and lugged it
into the store room at the back of the hall.
Even Winona hurried her exit, hoping to get
near the front of the queue for her school
dinner.

Daisy was tossing her yoghurt pot into the
store room over Jimmy's head when she
noticed that Nathan was still in his seat.
Instead of packing away his violin into the
case, he was sifting carefully through the
pages of his music.

'What's up?' Daisy asked, eyeing the

dinner ladies waiting impatiently behind their counter. The blinds had snapped up. They were in their overalls and caps, ready for action.

'Nothing,' Nathan muttered. He turned over each page and searched between them.

'Come along, Nathan!' Miss Ambler called, loaded down by recorders, triangles and maracas as she staggered towards the store room. 'Mr King wants us out of here!'

'Please Miss…' Nathan began softly. He ran a hand through his long, sticky-out hair, then crouched to look under his violin case.

'Not now, Nathan!' Ambler snapped back. 'Can't you see I'm busy?'

'But, Miss!' Nathan looked up with panic in his eyes.

'I *said*, not now!' she repeated, almost tripping over Jimmy as she barged into the dark storeroom.

So Nathan began to turf everything out of his bag.

Daisy saw maths books, bus tickets and an apple roll on to the floor.

In the distance, the dinner ladies rolled up their sleeves and advanced.

Then Nathan dipped his hand into his bag and drew out a jar.

Empty. Legs hadn't crawled back inside of his own free will.

Nathan's pale face crumpled and his hand began to tremble. But the wave of dinner ladies surrounded him and swept him away, clearing him up along with his violin and schoolbag. Before he knew it, poor Nathan, minus his beloved spider, was marooned outside the hall.

'What's up?' Jimmy asked Daisy as he came out of the storeroom.

'Have you seen Legs?' she demanded, dodging a dinner lady and re-checking the spot where Nathan had been sitting.

'No. Why?' Jimmy was puzzled. *Bang!* He ducked as another two strong-armed dinner ladies dumped a table into position.

'Because he's legged it, that's why!' Daisy told him.

Ducking and diving, Jimmy and Daisy made their way to the door.

'Legs has done *what*?' Jimmy demanded, glancing back at the rows of tables and newly set-out chairs.

'Legged it. Run away. Scarpered,' she repeated. 'And look at Nathan. He's falling apart!'

Two

For once, Daisy felt sorry for Know-All
Nathan.

OK, so he was super-brainy and he
collected bus tickets. He went to Saturday
morning Music Club. But he was human, like
the rest of them. She'd even seen tears in his
eyes as he stood in the queue for lunch.

'What's wrong with Nathan?' Jade asked
Daisy in a hushed voice.

'Legs did a runner,' Daisy explained.

'Legs has legged it!' The whisper passed down the line. 'Nathan's upset!'

'Move along!' the chief dinner lady barked.

The queue shuffled forward.

'I always knew it would happen one day!' Winona piped up from the front. 'I mean, how can you expect a spider to behave like a proper pet?'

'Sssshhh!' Daisy hissed.

Winona ignored her. 'A spider isn't like a dog, for instance. You can't exactly put an insect on a lead and expect to take it for walks!'

Nathan spun round. 'A spider isn't an insect!' he retorted. 'It's an arthropod. Anyone knows *that!*'

'Yeah!' Daisy echoed. 'A spider's an arth… arthur… thingy!'

Winona looked down her nose. 'All I'm saying is, I'm not surprised that Legs wandered off during our rehearsal.'

'Yeah, it was most likely the din you made

during your keyboard solo that put him off!' Jimmy put in.

Way to go, Jimmy! Sometimes Daisy's shy, soccer-mad best friend came out with things that surprised her. And he had shut Winona up at last.

'Don't worry, Nathan. Legs will show up.' Standing in line ahead of him, Jared offered words of comfort.

Nathan sniffed, then nodded. He hung his head and let the chief dinner lady herd him through the door back into the hall. Shuffling towards the counter, he didn't even bother to look around to see if he could spot his missing pet.

'I'm worried about him,' Daisy told Leonie. She knew how it felt to be parted from someone you loved. Once, she'd left Herbie her hamster in her school drawer over the weekend. Granted, Herbie was only a stuffed toy, but Daisy had been worried sick until she'd snuck in and rescued him. Then there was the time when Herbie had got lost in the

supermarket, and Daisy had dragged her
mum up and down the aisles looking for him.

They'd found him squatting amongst the
lettuces, his squidgy body half hidden by the
curly green leaves. Daisy had really told
Herbie off that time.

Leonie joggled Daisy's elbow. 'Look,
Nathan's not eating anything!' By this time
they had piled their plates high with cheese
pasties and chips and found seats opposite
the lonely figure.

'Have a chip!' Daisy offered, shoving her
plate towards him.

'No thanks. Not hungry,' he muttered back.

'You've got to eat something,' she
persisted, her own mouth full. 'And listen,
Jared's right. Legs will turn up soon.'

'He's never run away before.' Nathan's
bottom lip trembled. His fair hair stuck out at
wild angles where he'd pushed his fingers
through it. 'I can't understand why he did it.'

'Yeah, but that's not the point,' Leonie
jumped in. She always went right to the heart

of things and cut out the nonsense. 'The reason Legs ran away isn't important. What we have to do is FIND him!'

'Yeah!'

'Exactly!'

'Just what I was thinking!'

After lunch the gang got together in the playground to discuss Leonie's idea.

'We have to set up a search party!' Daisy told them, putting one arm around Jade's shoulder, the other around Jimmy's waist. They huddled together in a knot to make their secret plan.

'But don't let Nathan know what we're doing,' Leonie warned. 'In case it gets up his hopes.'

'OK,' the others agreed.

They all snuck a look at poor Nathan sitting on the step of the main entrance with his empty jam-jar beside him.

'How do you find a tiny spider in a huge school?' Winona wanted to know.

'Legs isn't tiny,' Daisy insisted. 'He's big for a spider. And at least we know where he was last seen.'

'Where?' Winona pressed.

'On Nathan's music stand, when he started to play the Strauss stuff.' Daisy recalled how Legs had seemed to dance on the page before he launched himself over the edge.

'Actually, Daisy, I don't think that was the last time Legs was seen,' Maya interrupted in her tiny voice.

It was as if a ghost had walked in. Maya was always there, with her long, smooth black hair tied in a neat ponytail, but she never spoke.

Winona, Daisy, Leonie, Jimmy, Jared and Jade turned to stare.

'What d'you mean?' Jared asked.

Maya cleared her throat and looked out from under her long, dark lashes. 'I think I saw Legs after that.'

'You did?'

'When?'

'Where?'

'Why didn't you say?'

'Ssshh!' Daisy instructed. 'Come on, Maya, tell us!'

'It was while we were queuing for dinner. I was standing by the secretary's office, where we all dump our bags when we go in to eat.'

'Yeah!' Daisy nodded. 'Are you saying you caught sight of the missing arth… arthur..'

'Arthropod,' Leonie chipped in.

'Maybe.' Maya said she couldn't be sure. 'I saw something move. A big black spider. It came creeping out of Winona's bag –'

'Yuck! Ugh! Oh, gross!' Winona wailed.

'Shut up, Winona!' the others hissed.

'– and out over the top of Jimmy's football, up on to the windowsill outside Mrs Hannam's office.' Maya finished her explanation and fell back into silence.

'Why didn't you say before?' Jared wanted to know.

'Because Maya didn't know Legs was missing until just now,' Daisy pointed out. 'It could've been any old spider crawling out of Winona's bag!'

'Ugh! Yuck! Don't!' Mizz Perfect screwed up her face and shuddered.

'So, this spider may or may not have been Legs.' Leonie frowned with concentration. 'But let's say that it was.'

'So we suspect that Legs spun a thread on to the floor during Nathan's solo and went exploring,' Daisy continued. 'He's busy munching a dead fly here and there, crawling in and out of people's bags.'

'My bag does NOT have dead flies in it!' Winona wailed.

'Quiet!' Leonie hissed.

'And before Legs knows it, Bernie King marches in and ends the lesson.' Daisy was determined to puzzle it out. 'Suddenly, he finds himself squeezed between Winona's pencil-case and hairbrush, say.'

'Oh, gross, gross, gross!' Winona broke free from the huddle and flounced off. 'I'm not going to listen any more!'

'So the poor spider tells himself he has to get out of the bag and find Nathan double-quick.' Daisy couldn't care less about Winona's tantrum. Anyway, things were easier to organise without the teacher's pet hanging around. 'He waits until the danger of being crushed to death on the spikes of a hairbrush passes – that is, until Winona dumps her bag outside Mrs Hannam's office – then he creeps out into the daylight.'

'And eventually he climbs up on to the windowsill!' Leonie nodded. She thought they were on to something and turned back to Maya. 'Was it that window with the sliding section which you push back to speak to the person in the office?'

Maya nodded. 'The window was open at the time.'

'Hmm.' Daisy thought hard. They had to be clever about this and not rush in.

Point one – It seemed Legs had legged it towards the secretary's office.

Point two – Mrs Hannam's room was strictly out of bounds to pupils.

Point three – everyone was scared stiff of Hannam the Horror with her helmet of blonde hair and blood-red lips.

'Hmm what?' Jimmy asked. As usual, he trusted Daisy to come up with the answer.

'Hmmmmm.' In fact, she didn't have a clue what to do next. And anyway, the bell for the start of school had just gone. The group broke up and they sprinted for the door,

'Leave it to me!' Daisy muttered to Jimmy as they raced for the classroom. 'I'll think of something!'

Brilliant! Daisy was feeling pleased with herself. She'd cunningly escaped from literacy hour and stood poised to ring Mrs Hannam's bell.

She'd worked out the perfect excuse.

Ten minutes into the lesson, she'd started to sniffle.

Quietly at first – *sniff-sniff* – then louder – *snuffle-snuffle* – until Ambler had looked up from the pile of books on her desk.

'Daisy Morelli, if your nose is running, use a tissue!'she'd snapped.

Sniffle-sniffle. Daisy had sat head down, hiding behind her hair.

'Please Miss, it's not that!' Leonie had spoken up for her. 'I think she's crying!'

'Daisy Morelli crying?' Rambler Ambler had stood up in a state of shock and come to the

back of the class. She'd stared hard at
Daisy's face.

Sniff-sniff-sob. With a lot of effort, Daisy
had even managed to force real tears down
her cheeks.

'Whatever is the matter?' the teacher had
asked.

The thing about Ambler was that she was
easily fooled.

Daisy had hung her head. 'Please Miss,
my baby sister Mia is sick!' *Snuffle-sob.*

Definitely
30
Daisy

'Oh dear! Oh dear, dear!' Miss Ambler had fallen for it straight away. 'Is the poor little thing very ill?'

'Miss, she might have to go to hospital.' Daisy had laid it on thick. 'My mum was taking her to the doctor this morning. I'm really worried about her, Miss!'

'Try not to get upset. I'm sure Mia's going to be all right.' Ambler had thought for a while, then said, 'Is there anything we can do?'

'Please Miss, I'd feel better if I could go to Mrs Hannam's office and ring my mum to find out how Mia is.' Daisy had put on her saddest voice, her fingers tightly crossed under her desk.

'Yes, dear. I understand.' Ambler had nodded kindly. 'I think that's a very good idea. In fact, why don't you run along to the office right this minute!'

Drring! Daisy pressed the secretary's bell loud and clear. Now was her chance to follow up Maya's last sighting of Legs.

Across the entrance lobby, inside the hall, Bernie King helped the dinner ladies to clear the lunch-time tables.

'Yes?' Mrs Hannam's blonde head appeared at the sliding window.

'Erm…' Clearing her throat gave Daisy time to scan the windowsill and the counter beyond. There were piles of paper, envelopes, books and lists – but no big, furry spiders.

'Come along!' Mrs Hannam was a busy woman. She had letters to type.

'Erm… please could I use the phone?' Daisy's laser-sharp gaze took in the secretary's cluttered desk, her computer, the bright red jacket which she'd slung over the back of her swivel-chair.

'Did Miss Ambler give you permission?'

'Erm… yes.' Daisy's eyes were glued to the red jacket. It had black buttons and a black embroidered pattern right down the front. Part of the pattern seemed to be moving…

'Very well.' Mrs Hannam opened the door

to let Daisy in. Then she headed back to her computer.

'Erm!' Daisy squeaked. The black scrawly bit on the secretary's jacket was definitely on the move.

'The phone's over there.' Hannam the Horror pointed a red fingernail towards a cluttered shelf. Her red high heels made small dents in the grey carpet as she walked.

'Thanks!' Daisy croaked. That moving scrawly bit was Legs! He was taking a quiet stroll across Hannam's jacket, minding his own business.

Daisy's luck was in. Her very first attempt to find the runaway spider had come good. Now all she had to do was corner Legs and capture him.

Wow, will Nathan be pleased! she thought, forgetting all about the fake phone call and creeping quietly towards Hannam's chair.

Three

'Aaaaaggghhhh!' Mrs Hannam gave a terrible cry.

She clutched at Daisy and dug her long nails into her arms.

Two steps away from her chair she'd spotted Legs crawling up her jacket.

'Le'go!' Daisy spluttered.

Hannam hugged her close.

'Ouch! Aagh! That hurts!'

The secretary tightened her grip still more. 'Ugh! How disgusting!'

Legs had come to a sudden halt. He seemed to be trying to work out what was making the dreadful noise.

'Help!' Daisy cried, deep in the grip of Hannam's red claws.

'Uuuugghhh!' Hannam wailed. 'I can't stand spiders. Look at the great, ugly thing. It's staring straight at me!'

'Help!' Daisy croaked again.

And then the door flew open and Bernie King came crashing in.

'What happened? Where's the fire? Who's dying?' he roared.

'Help!' Daisy squeaked. Hannam's nails were digging right into her and her breath was almost gone. 'Tell her to *let go*!'

The caretaker spied Daisy going weak at the knees. 'I might have known,' he grunted. 'It's Daisy blooming Morelli causing trouble again!'

'Help!' she sighed weakly.

'Oh, Mr King!' Mrs Hannam suddenly let go of Daisy and tried to grab the caretaker instead.

'Now, steady on!' Bernie said, backing away. He almost stepped on Lennox, who was close on his heels as always.

The bulldog growled and blundered against Mrs Hannam's chair, bringing her red jacket down on top of him.

'Aaaaggghhh!' The secretary saw the jacket land on Lennox's squat body and made a run for the door.

'Grab him!' Daisy gasped at Bernie. 'Quick, before Legs runs away again!'

As Lennox turned blindly beneath the jacket and the caretaker hesitated, Daisy saw that it was up to her. She would have to make a heroic rugby tackle on Fat Lennox and whisk Legs away with her bare hands.

So she spread her arms wide and crouched low, ready to pounce.

Lennox growled and snapped beneath the jacket.

'What's this about Legs?' asked a confused Bernie King.

'Legs is Nathan Moss's spider, and he's on my jacket!' Mrs Hannam shrieked as she completed her exit and slammed the door behind her.

Ready – steady – Daisy took a deep breath. *Go!* She leaped at Lennox.

Grrrrrrgh! The bulldog made a blind charge under Mrs Hannam's desk.

Umph! Daisy missed and landed on the grey carpet with a heavy thump.

'A spider on Mrs Hannam's jacket, eh?' A dim light had gone on inside Bernie's head. He seized a nearby newspaper and rolled it up. Then he held it in the air like a sword.

'Wait!' Daisy pleaded as she struggled back to her feet. 'Legs is Nathan's pet. Don't splat him!'

Whack! Bernie ignored her. He thumped the roll of newspaper down on to the jacket.

'Grruggh!' Lennox barked and shot free of the desk. The jacket lay still on the carpet.

Whack! Whack! Whack! Bernie King thumped it three more times.

Splat! Daisy cringed as she pictured the result. 'Don't! Nathan loves Legs!' she cried.

'Blooming thing!' Bernie grunted as the fat spider scampered out from under the desk.

Daisy breathed again. The caretaker had missed by a mile.

Legs looked this way and that. He spied Bernie breathing heavily and Lennox drooling by the door. So he sprinted across the carpet and up a white net curtain until he reached the ceiling.

Cool! Daisy admired Legs's speed. There he was, perched on the pelmet, peering down.

'Drat!' Bernie King flung down his newspaper then craned his neck to see where the spider had got to. 'Ah, there it is!'

'Leave him. He's not doing any harm,' Daisy said. As soon as things calmed down, she would be able to step in and rescue Legs. 'Look, he's spinning a thread and coming down already!' They watched as the spider launched himself from the pelmet. He dropped halfway to the floor, wiggled his eight legs, then climbed back up. *Weeee-wiggle-wiggle-up!* Quick as a flash. Bernie had tried to get him as he spun down, but once more had grabbed thin air.

Daisy grinned to herself. Legs obviously had a sense of humour.

'Mrs Hannam, fetch me my step-ladders!' Bernie yelled through the closed door. 'I'll get the little nuisance if it's the last thing I do!'

Back on the pelmet, Legs decided to play the game over again. *Weeee-wiggle-grab(miss)-up!*

'Hey, he's bungee-jumping!' Daisy laughed.

...*'To the max!' she called from the bottom of the giant cliff.*

Legs loved taking risks, but this was a big one even for him. He looked down at the three hundred foot drop and the jagged rocks below. Beyond the rocks,

giant waves crashed against the shore.
Above his head, seagulls whirled.

'To the max! To the max!' the crowd
chanted faintly, their voices carried off by
the wind.

'Come on, Legs, you can do it!' Daisy
urged. Her voice rose above the rest.
'You're the best!'

Legs heard her and gritted his teeth.
Sure, he could bungee jump better than
anyone in the world. But was this one
jump too far? Once more, he stared
down at the dizzy drop and his eight legs
started to tremble and shake.

'To the max, Legs!' Daisy cried...

'So, Bernie tried to reach him with the step-
ladder,' Daisy told her dad later that evening,
her dark eyes sparkling as she described
Legs's mega-jump. 'But every time he
climbed up the steps, Legs bungee-jumped
to safety on his invisible thread. Bernie
got redder and redder and more and more

out of breath!'

Gianni thumped pizza dough down on to a board. He pushed and slapped it into shape. 'This Legs, he is a friend of yours?'

'No, Dad!' Daisy tutted and scooped some grated cheese from a bowl. 'Legs is a *spider*. Haven't you been listening?'

Gianni shrugged. He slapped and flipped the dough. 'A spider, huh? So the take-carer...'

'...The Care-Taker!'

'*Si*. The Take-Carer, he cannot catch the spider. So he gives up in the end?'

'*Si*. I mean, yes!' Daisy grinned from ear to ear. 'Bernie was really mad. He had smoke coming out of his ears!'

'And did you catch the spider yourself, Daisy mia?' With a blast of hot air, Gianni opened an oven door and took out a freshly baked pizza.

'Ah, well, no. Not exactly,' she confessed.

'I give in!' Bernie King had admitted defeat

at last.

Legs had laughed down at them from the top of the pelmet.

Bernie and Lennox had stomped off together. Daisy had peered out of the office to find out what had happened to Mrs Hannam.

'I refuse to go back in until that spider has been caught!' the secretary was telling Mrs Waymann, the headteacher, in the corridor.

Daisy ducked back into the room, but too late. Mrs Eagle-Eye Waymann had spotted her.

And she was sent back to her classroom.

'Go!' Mrs Waymann's voice had boomed out when Daisy had tried to argue.

'B-b-but...!' *What about Legs?*

'Now!' Waymann had insisted. Daisy had taken one last quick glance up at the pelmet...

'And guess what? Legs had legged it again!' Daisy told her dad with a mouthful of cheese.

Gianni put the cooked pizza into a box and tied the box with ribbon. He slid the whole thing through a hatch for Angie to give to a customer. 'So he escaped after all this?'

Daisy nodded, then sighed. 'Poor Nathan.'

'Is Nathan playing in the concert this Thursday?' Angie asked as she finished serving and came into the kitchen.

'Yep.' Another mouthful of cheese glued Daisy's tongue to the top of her mouth.

'Ah, the concert!' Gianni dusted flour from his hands on to his striped apron. He pointed

to the two tickets pinned to the noticeboard beside the fridge. 'This will be a proud moment for the Morellis!'

'Hmm.' Daisy made rapid tracks for the door. *Big mistake!*

Last Sunday she'd been talking about the concert over breakfast and made a massive thing of her part in the show. Now, somehow, her dad thought she was the star!

'Daisy Morelli is singing a solo!' Gianni beamed fondly after her as she swung out of the kitchen. 'My Daisy, my little Italian opera star!'

'I can't tell Dad the truth!' Daisy had gone up to her bedroom and decided to tell Herbie everything.

Why not? The squidgy toy hamster didn't say a word as he perched on her pillow. He didn't have to. She knew exactly what he was thinking.

'Because he's really looking forward to the concert. You know what my dad's like. He loves music. And I couldn't bear the look on his face if I had to tell him I'm only playing yoghurt pots with Year 2!'

But he'll find out anyway! Herbie winked wisely with his one eye.

'I know!' Daisy sighed. 'To tell you the truth, I wish this stupid concert wasn't happening at all!'

'Everything OK?' Angie asked, poking her head around the door.

'Fine!' Daisy fibbed.

'You sure?' Her mum came into the room, her head to one side. 'You don't look fine. Are you certain you're not worried about something?'

Tell her! Herbie urged. *She'll understand!*

Daisy grabbed the hamster and shoved him under her pillow.

'I'm OK, honest!' She insisted.

Mmm-umm-phuh-ugh! ('Hey, no need to take it out on me!') Herbie cried.

I only lied to Dad about singing a solo! Daisy desperately wished she could confide in her mum. But she couldn't.

Witch Waymann only shouted at me. Horrid Hannam only squeezed me to death. Bernie King only blamed me for everything. Lennox only nearly bit my hand off. Oh, and Legs has only run away... AGAIN!

Four

'What do we know about spiders?' Leonie
asked as she and Daisy queued for
assembly first thing next morning.

Daisy trusted Leonie to do some sharp
thinking over the problem of Legs. That was
why they were talking hard as they shuffled
forward into the hall.

'They have eight legs. They're arthur – o –
thingies…' She came up with the first facts

that entered her head.

'No, I don't mean the science stuff.' Leonie spoke without moving her lips. It was one of her most useful tricks.

On guard by the door, Miss Ambler heard whispering and gave the whole class a warning look.

'I mean, what do we know about the way Legs is likely to behave?'

'Right! Well, if it was down to me, I'd hide!'

Leonie agreed. 'He'd go undercover in case Bernie tried to splat him again. OK, what else?'

'Ssshhh!' Miss Ambler warned, still not able to spot who was talking. She looked even more worried and worn down than usual, her arms loaded with piles of sheet-music, with a pair of maracas and a tambourine wobbling on top.

'I expect I'd be hungry, so I'd spin a web and try to catch flies.'

Leonie thought for a while. 'Right. So that's spiders in general. But what about Legs in particular? What's special about Nathan's spider?'

'Hmm.' It was Daisy's turn to concentrate. 'OK. Legs likes high places. He enjoys looking down on people to see what's going on…'

'Jared and Kyle, stop talking!' Miss Ambler guessed wrong.

'Miss, it's not us!' they protested. Kyle gave Daisy a dirty look. The queue shuffled forward another couple of steps.

'Please, Miss!' Nathan piped up. He was right at the front, looking pale and pasty. His sticky-up hair had flopped over his forehead.

'Not now, Nathan!' the teacher snapped. 'Wait until after assembly.'

Poor Nathan sighed. Without Legs crawling up his sleeve or along his shoulder, he looked lonely and lost.

'…And Legs likes to have a joke,' Daisy went on. 'Y'know; he dangles in front of you, then – boing! – he bounces up out of reach.' The *boing* came out louder than she'd planned. Miss Ambler shot her a suspicious look.

'So, he's clever,' Leonie muttered. 'And he's active; a pretty fit spider as a matter of fact.'

The queue shuffled on into the hall. Miss Ambler's gaze was fixed on Daisy.

... 'To the max, Legs!' Daisy yelled.

The super-fit spider had moved from one extreme sport to another. He'd grown bored with bungee jumping. Now it was tight-rope walking.

Legs took a deep breath. The rope stretched out in front of him, all the way across the Niagara Falls. If he missed his footing and fell, the giant waterfall would swoosh him away.

And it was a long, long way to the other side...

'Legs could do anything he wanted to!' Daisy said out loud, right under Miss Ambler's nose.

The teacher pounced. 'Daisy Morelli, it was you all along! Typical! You can't keep your tongue still for a single moment!'

Daisy cringed while Leonie breezed on into assembly.

'Very well, Daisy, since you can't obey the Silence-in-Assembly rule, you must stay back during lunch break. And you can help me set up the music stands for this afternoon's rehearsal!' Ambler decided. Frazzled and worried witless about Thursday's concert, she told Daisy she wouldn't hear another word!

Cool! For once Daisy didn't mind missing lunchtime play. In fact, things were working out perfectly.

Leonie was outside with Jimmy, Maya,

Jared and Jade. The girl-who-never-got-caught was in charge of the main search party, while Daisy planned to go solo on a secret inside raid.

'We'll take the playground, the bike shed and the yard outside Bernie King's office,' Leonie had promised. Her brown eyes shone with excitement under her halo of curly brown hair. 'If Legs has come out into the open, don't worry we'll find him!'

'Well, we'd better make it soon.' Jimmy had pointed at Nathan, who was sitting alone at the lunch tables for the second day running. He was picking at his food, refusing to talk to anybody. 'Poor old Nathan can't take much more.'

So they'd set off on their search, leaving Daisy to do chores for Ambler.

'Wait here!' The teacher had grabbed her before she'd even finished her pudding and hauled her off to stand outside the secretary's office while she went in to speak to Mrs Hannam.

And now Daisy was working out exactly how she could escape from the chores in the hall and find some time to pick up the Legs trail once more.

She would have to be smart. She would seize a moment when Ambler was too busy to notice that she had sneaked off – maybe when the teacher was in the little storeroom at the back of the hall. She would have a story ready in case she got caught.

…'The name's Morelli. Daisy Morelli.'

'Mizz Morelli. Delighted to meet you at last.' The fat, bald man was dressed in a smart, dark suit. He wore a heavy gold ring and aimed a snug silver gun between Daisy's eyes.

'Likewise, Mr Diamond,' Daisy replied. She noted the glint of a small white gem set into a front tooth as Diamond's thin lips stretched into a cruel smile.

It was a lie. In fact, this was the very man she'd been hoping never to meet.

Especially not on the roof of a twenty storey building, with no way down and a gun pointing right at her.

'Then it's a pity our meeting is going to be so short.'

The fat man laughed as his finger squeezed the trigger.

Quick as a flash, Daisy pressed the button on her secret weapon. A laser beam shot from her wristwatch and zapped the gun right out of Diamond's hand.

The enemy spymaster yelped and reeled back over the edge of the tower block. He screamed as he fell...

Rambler Ambler came out of Mrs Hannam's office. Her eyes lit on Daisy as if she'd forgotten all about her lunchtime punishment. 'Ah yes, come with me into the hall. You can carry the music stands out of the storeroom and set them up ready for this afternoon.'

Daisy dragged along behind the teacher.

She scuffed her worn trainers and made the soles squeak on the polished floor.

'Oh, Nathan!' Miss Boring-Snoring exclaimed. She'd overlooked him too until this moment, when she spied him standing by the door, his violin case at his feet. 'Yes dear, I know you don't feel well enough to go out to play. So just sit quietly and read your Strauss music, there's a good boy.'

Yes dear, no dear – there's a good boy! Daisy mouthed the words behind Miss Ambler's back.

Nathan slumped down in a chair and sighed.

The teacher turned to Daisy. 'And you, Daisy Morelli, can run back to Mrs Hannam's office and fetch me the key to the storeroom. I forgot to collect it when I called in just now.'

'Yes miss!' Daisy turned and ran.

Cool again! Just the chance she needed to have a bit of a snoop to see if she could pick up Legs' trail.

Slipping out of the door, Daisy checked both ways to see if the coast was clear. The entrance hall was empty, and so was the corridor leading to the office, with the headteacher's room beyond. Dropping into a crouch, she made her way past Mrs Hannam's sliding window.

Where would a nimble spider go after he got fed up bungee-jumping from a pelmet? Would he stay high and find a corner of the office to make a nice web in? Or would he go exploring?

Click! A door opened further down the corridor. Daisy heard the secretary's voice from inside Mrs Waymann's room.

'Yes, Mrs Waymann!' Horrid Hannam backed out of the room in her high heels. 'I'll see to that straight away.'

Daisy had only a split second to decide what to do. Rather than face the blonde battleaxe, she decided to dive for the nearest door; the one marked "Staff Toilet". Quickly opening it, she darted inside.

Trippety-trip-trip! Hannam clicked along
the corridor.

Daisy held her breath. In the tiny,
windowless room she could make out a
white wash-basin, a holder for paper towels,
coats hanging on pegs and a second door
which must lead into the loo. The whole
place smelt of pine air-freshener, mixed with
a faint whiff of Mrs Waymann's special
perfume.

Trippety-trip! The secretary's footsteps
passed safely by. Daisy could breathe again.

And now that she was in the cloakroom,
she might as well take a proper look around.
A nice shady spot like this might be just the
sort of place Legs would choose to spend a
night. Hey, and there was a link with
Hannam's room next door! A water pipe
went straight through the wall from the office
to the cloakroom. *And* there was a crack in
the plaster that a spider could easily creep
through!

Daisy felt she was getting warm. She started to look more closely – under the sink, behind the coats, hoping to find a definite clue. A bluebottle buzzed out from behind the coats and flew straight into the mirror above the sink. Dazed, it fell into the bowl. Daisy watched it pick itself up and fly again. This time it headed in a crooked path towards the ceiling, where it caught its legs in a big spider's web.

Wow! Hey! Wow! Daisy gasped. She turned on the light to see better. The web wasn't just big. It was humungous! A Legs-sized web!

The fly struggled and managed to pull itself free. It buzzed close to the light hanging from the ceiling. Daisy followed its unsteady course. The bluebottle came to rest on a loop of black wire trailing from the light.

Aagh! Dizzy fly came face to face with the maker of the web.

'Legs!' Daisy cried.

Nathan's spider perched on the wire like a

circus acrobat. Huge and fat with long hairy legs, there was no mistaking him. The dazed fly saw Legs and took a dive from the high wire back towards the sink.

Daisy's heart beat fast. This time she would catch him!

Clickety-click-click! Before Daisy had time to make a move, a second pair of footsteps came down the corridor. They were heavier than Hannam's and they stopped outside the door. The handle turned. There was a strong smell of perfume. Daisy flung herself at the row of pegs and hid behind the coats. She was invisible except for a pair of skinny legs and scruffy trainers.

'Hmmm!' Mrs Waymann came in. She hummed a little tune and checked her reflection in the mirror. 'Ttt-ttt!' she murmured. 'Who's been leaving the light on? I must have a word with
Mrs Hannam about that.'

Behind the coats, Daisy tried not to

breathe. *Go away!* she prayed. *Please turn the light off and go!*

'Dum-dah, tiddle-dum!' The headteacher pulled a lipstick from her bag. She got her lips into position close to the mirror.

And this was when Legs got careless.

He'd seen the bluebottle spiral down towards the floor. *Late lunch!* he'd thought. And with Waymann's lips just inches from the mirror, he'd bungee-jumped down to the sink.

Daisy saw him do it. Peeping out from behind the coats, she saw him launch himself from the wire and spin himself a thread. She saw Waymann open her mouth in surprise and almost swallow the giant spider.

'Oh!' she gasped, watching Legs drop in front of her face.

With split-second timing, the headmistress raised her hand to break the thread.

Legs went into free fall. He landed in the sink.

Waymann went

for the tap. She turned it on before Legs had time to realise what was happening.

Water gushed out. It caught the spider in its sudden flood. It swirled him around and pushed him towards the plug hole.

'Shoo!' Waymann cried, giving the water an extra swish.

Glug-glug! The plug hole sucked water into the waste pipe.

Daisy saw Legs curl into a ball and get swept along. He was drawn into tighter circles, closer to the hole.

Oh no! She clenched her jaw to stop herself from crying out.

'Good riddance!' Wayman heard the final glug as Legs vanished from view. 'We can't have nasty spiders building webs in the school wherever they choose!'

No! Daisy couldn't bear to look. *Glug! Sccchluck! Gone!*

The Head turned off the tap then jammed the plug firmly into the hole. 'And don't come back!' she said.

Gone! Daisy swallowed hard. She heard the suck of the water down the drain.

Gone forever! Legs was no more!

Five

*'You don't love me maybe,
But just supposing I love you!'*

Gianni Morelli sang at the top of his voice.

Daisy could hear him in the bathroom, singing and shaving, getting ready for another busy day in the Pizza Palazzo.

*'Da-dum da-dum da-da
Da da-da-da-da dum da-dum!'*

He finished shaving and poked his head

into Daisy's room. 'So you want to keep your song a secret!' he grinned. 'You like to give your papa a BIG surprise, hey?'

Daisy ducked her head and pretended to look for her trainers under the bed.

Tell him! Herbie hissed.

Shut up! She reached up to the pillow and stuffed the truth-loving hamster into her schoolbag. She velcroed it tightly shut.

Hey! Herbie squeaked. *You'll be sorry. And don't say I didn't warn you!*

Gianni came into the room. 'Why don't you give me a tiny *little* clue, huh? C'mon. Is it a song from an opera like Carmen? Or is it a modern song like Madonna sings?'

'Not telling!' Daisy muttered.

'Ah, a secret!' Her dad grinned. 'Daisy wants to keep it a surprise! So, anyway. Tomorrow night we'll all know the answer, eh?'

Yeah, she's playing yoghurt-pot drums with Year 2! Herbie said in a muffled voice from inside the bag.

'You don't love me maybe…' Gianni went downstairs, singing happily.

What am I gonna do? Daisy sighed into thin air.

Tell him the truth! Herbie cried in a tiny voice.

Daisy put her hands over her ears. *'Da-dum da-dum da-da …'*

'So what did Nathan say when you told him that Legs had vanished down the plug-hole?' Jimmy asked Daisy as they walked to school together.

It was a drizzly, windy day, but Jimmy was dressed as always in his short-sleeved football shirt and shorts.

'He didn't say much,' Daisy admitted.

She'd waited for Waymann to touch up her lipstick and give herself a squirt from her handy perfume bottle. Ten seconds after the headteacher had left the cloakroom, Daisy had edged out into the corridor and tiptoed back to the hall.

'I knew I had to break it to him straight away,' she told Jimmy. 'He was sitting there in the hall, staring into space. Legs's empty jam-jar was on the seat next to him.'

'Phuh!' Jimmy sighed hopelessly. 'Rather you than me. So what did he say?'

'Nothing,' Daisy reported. 'He just picked up the jam-jar and looked at it.'

'Did you tell him everything?'

Daisy shook her head. 'No. I spared him the details. I mean, how would you feel if you heard your favourite pet had been splooshed down a drain? So I just told him that Waymann had found Legs in the loo. And that was that.'

Everyone in the school knew that Waymann might look soft and cuddly and smell like a perfume shop, but underneath she was hard as nails. If she'd found Legs, Nathan would know that the spider never stood a chance.

* * *

..."Rest in peace, Legs!"

Daisy wore a long black veil and stood quietly while Nathan fixed a small wooden cross into the ground. She understood that though there was no body, he wanted something to remember his spider by.

The rest of the gang were gathered to pay their respects – Jimmy, Leonie, Jade, Maya, Jared, even Kyle and Winona. They stood with bowed heads, faces

covered by black veils hands clasped in
front of them.

'I've written a poem,' Nathan
whispered, pulling a smudged sheet of
paper out of his pocket. 'Do you mind if I
read it?' They shook their heads.

'"Farewell To Legs,"' he began. '"A
Boy's Best Friend!"'

Daisy stared down at the small cross.
She felt her throat go tight as Nathan
read from the crumpled paper.

'"Why did we have to say goodbye,
Knowing how much it would make me
                                    cry?
Why do I have to feel this way,
Knowing there was still so much to
                                    say?"'

'Uh-huh-huh-huh!' Maya was the first
to cry. Then Winona. Then Kyle and
Jade.

Daisy swallowed hard. Nathan read on
but she hardly heard a word. When he
finished, Leonie stepped forward.

'We'll miss Legs too,' she told Nathan. 'Not as much as you, obviously. But we will miss him.'

And that was it. The lump in Daisy's throat grew enormous and she could no longer hold back the tears...

'Hey, Jimmy. Hey, Daisy,' Leonie said when she joined them at the park gates. Her face was glum as she too thought of having to face Nathan when they reached school.

Daisy pictured the front page headlines in Spider News: DAREDEVIL SPIDER DROWNS! LEGS LOST DOWN PLUGHOLE! The disaster would shake the whole spider world.

'Hey, everyone.' Winona joined them at the end of Woodbridge Road. 'How's Nathan? Does anyone know?'

'How d'you expect him to be?' Leonie replied. 'Anyway, hush. There he is now.'

Nathan was walking through the school gates. He looked like he was in a dream. A bad dream.

'How's he gonna to be able to play in the concert tomorrow night?' Jimmy whispered. 'And he's one of the main people!'

'Don't worry, I can play *two* pieces.' Winona stepped in quickly. 'Hmm. Maybe I should suggest that to Miss Ambler, just in case!'

'Win – oh – na!' the others cried.

'What?' She stared back at them, wide-eyed. 'I was only trying to help!'

'Well don't!' Daisy snapped. 'How about cheering poor Nathan up, instead?

'What now, Winona?' Miss Ambler demanded at the start of the afternoon rehearsal. She'd spent the whole morning quietly going mad.

'We'll never have enough yoghurt pots for all of Year 2!' she'd bleated suddenly during what was supposed to be a science lesson. And, 'What am I going to do if there aren't enough seats for everyone to sit on?' during maths. Strands of the teacher's wispy hair had fallen over her face while she'd searched wildly for her glasses. 'Miss, you're wearing them!' Winona had called out from the front row.

Lunch had come and gone. Ambler had trotted here and there, searching for empty yoghurt pots and losing her music. And now Winona Jones had gone out to the front just when they were about to start the run-through.

'Please, Miss, Nathan says he doesn't feel very well again!'

'Yes, I know, dear. Don't bother me just now.'

'But Miss Ambler!' Winona stood her ground. Now was the time when she could suggest practising an extra solo, just in case.

Daisy fiddled with her yoghurt pots and frowned. *Trust Winona Stupid Jones!* She glanced at Nathan, who still seemed to have a vacant, lost look in his eyes. He hadn't even opened his violin case, ready to rehearse.

'Not now, Winona!' Ambler turned away to fumble with her music. 'Has anyone seen my glasses?' she wailed.

'Miss, they're on top of your head,' Winona said calmly.

'Thank you, Winona, and sit down!' Miss Ambler screeched. She was a millimetre away from totally losing it. 'If we don't begin right this second, we're never going to be ready!'

Eeek! Plink-plonk! Boom! Bop-bop!

It was no good; the opening number was as bad as ever.

Miss Ambler tore out what was left of her hair. 'No, no, no! Jimmy and Daisy, you only come in with the drum after the recorders and guitar have finished!'

Boom! Jimmy's hand twitched.

Bop! Daisy copied.

'Sorry, Miss,' they muttered.

'Oh, I give up! Goodness only knows what it will sound like when we have the whole of Year 2 trying to follow you two on their yoghurt pots!' Ambler looked really down in the dumps. She turned to Winona for rescue.

'Play your keyboard solo while Jimmy and Daisy sort themselves out.'

Winona tossed back her fair curls and played.

'Well done, dear. At least I know I can rely on you.' Ambler glared at Daisy and Jimmy as she spoke.

Eeeeak! Maya blew spit out of the end of her recorder.

Plonk! Leonie strummed her guitar.

Winona shot up her hand to suggest

playing an extra piece.

'Not now, dear,' Ambler waved her away and turned to Nathan.

'Let me hear your nice waltz now,' she told him.

'Miss, I don't think I can play,' he sighed. His violin was still in its case. His freckled face was pale and hollow.

'What's the matter? Are you still ill?' Ambler panicked.

Nathan sagged. He hung his head.

'Miss, his pet spider got killed,' Winona told the teacher for him. 'Mrs Waymann found him in the staff toilet...'

'Dear, dear, dear!' Rambler Ambler was at a loss. 'I'm sorry to hear it, Nathan. But surely you can get over a little thing like that in time for the concert?'

'He can't, Miss!' Winona insisted. 'But I could...'

'Later, Winona!' Ambler cut her short with a savage rap of her conducting stick. 'Be quiet, all of you and let me think!'

* * *

'She's in a real tizz,' Leonie said as she stored her guitar in the small room after the rehearsal had finished.

'She's gone totally nuts,' Daisy agreed, helping Jimmy to lug the big drum out of the hall.

'She hasn't a clue what to do about Nathan getting sick,' Jimmy added.

They all looked over their shoulders at the grieving boy.

'All over some stupid spider!' Winona said in a loud voice, sulking because she still hadn't got her own way.

Nathan heard her. He winced and turned away.

'Sssshhh!' Daisy warned.

But Winona didn't care if Nathan overheard. 'Legs was only a spider!' she insisted. 'I don't see why he's so upset!'

'Da-dum da-dum da-da – but just supposing I love you!' Daisy sang out in a voice loud enough to drown out Winona's

whingeing. It was the first thing that came into her head. *'You don't love me maybe, but just supposing da-da-dum!'*

'Who was that?' Miss Ambler burst out of the storeroom.

'Da-dum da-dum...' By this time Daisy was belting out her dad's favourite tune. She didn't see or hear Ambler until too late.

'Daisy!' the teacher gasped. 'Was that you?'

Winona grinned. Daisy was about to get into big trouble for making so much noise.

'I love you!' Daisy trilled.

She only stopped when Jimmy gave her a warning jab in the ribs.

'But that's wonderful!' Ambler sighed. She looked in amazement at the red-faced singer. 'Daisy Morelli, I'd *no idea* you had such a beautiful voice!'

Six

It was the day of the concert. Legs was dead and Daisy was to sing a solo. How had it happened?

Fast; that was how.

When Boring Snoring had caught Daisy singing an opera tune in order to drown out Winona, she'd grabbed her and given her the third degree.

'How long have you been able to sing

like that?'

'Why didn't you tell me?'

'Do you know all of the words?'

Daisy had been too gobsmacked to reply.

'Yes she does, Miss Ambler,' Leonie had stepped in. (Leonie would have said to anything to prevent Winona from grabbing a second solo.) 'I've heard her sing the whole thing. And, as it happens, I can play it on the guitar!'

'Oh!' Miss Ambler had clasped her hands together as if her prayers had been answered. 'Oh, Leonie... Daisy, dear – if Nathan isn't well enough to perform tomorrow night, do you think you could possibly save the day?'

'Thanks a bunch!' Later, on the way home, Daisy had blamed Winona for everything.

'What did I do?' Winona was confused. Daisy felt double-crossed without exactly being able to put her finger on how. 'You got me into a fine mess, that's what you did.

Now I have to stand up in front of two
hundred people and warble some silly song,
and it's all down to you!'

The two girls had parted with black looks.

But at least Daisy had been able to take
Herbie out of her schoolbag with a told-you-
so stare. 'See!' she said, dumping him on her
pillow. 'I get to sing a stupid solo after all!'

Herbie said nothing.

'At least Dad'll be pleased,' Daisy grunted.

And Gianni went on and on about the
concert all that evening. He told every
customer who came in for pizza that his
Daisy was going to be an opera star. He and
Angie were taking the evening off work to go
to school and watch.

'We have a babysitter for Mia, and Jimmy
Black's older sister, Charlotte, is going to run
the restaurant until we get back,' Angie
explained. 'I must say, Gianni and I are really
looking forward to it!'

Daisy cringed each time she heard it. She
couldn't bear her dad singing *You-don't-*

love-me under his breath as he chopped tomatoes and mixed them with herbs.

Finally, she went upstairs to bed.

'Nervous?' Angie asked when she popped her head around the door to say goodnight. 'Don't worry, it's only natural. I'm sure you'll be absolutely fine.'

Daisy groaned and buried her head under the pillow. If only she hadn't opened her big mouth to hum. But then it was news to her that she could sing. Nobody had ever mentioned it before... Anyway, maybe Nathan would be better in time... But then he would play the violin and she'd be stuck on yoghurt pots... her dad would know she'd lied...

Tossing and turning, dreading Thursday evening, Daisy eventually drifted off to sleep.

'Now, Year 2, remember to do exactly what Daisy Morelli does on her yoghurt pot!' Miss Ambler gave the order loud and clear.

The little ones sat cross legged at the front

holding their home-made drums.

It was the final rehearsal. Only four hours to go before the real thing. Somehow the teacher had held herself together and was making one last big effort. She held up her stick. 'Ready – *And!*'

Boom-boom, boppa-bop, boom-boom, eeeek!

'Better!' Ambler said faintly at the end of the opening number. 'Very good, Year 2. Now you can line up at the door and go quietly back to Mrs Hunt's class!'

The little ones queued with shiny faces. Tonight was their big night.

Then it was Winona's turn. Daisy could see from her face that even Mizz Perfect was nervous. As for Daisy, her hands were sweating and her throat was dry.

Maybe Nathan would soon feel better! She stole a quick look at him. Nope; Nathan looked as pasty as ever. He was staring at his hands, thinking his own gloomy thoughts.

Brrum-brrum-be-deedly... dum! Winona

fumbled her tune.

A shudder ran through Miss Ambler. 'Try again,' she said sharply.

Brrum-brrum-be-dee… Another stumble. Winona looked worried and started again.

'Hmmm.' At the end of the solo, Miss Ambler sounded wobbly.

'Never mind. I'm sure it'll be all right tonight.' And, as Winona sat down, the teacher moved on to Nathan.

Nathan shook his head.

'We'll try later,' Ambler said as kindly as she could. Then she turned to Daisy.

Daisy's legs trembled. Her mouth felt dry as sandpaper. She couldn't move.

'Stand up!' Leonie hissed. She arranged her guitar and got ready to play.

Daisy stood. Didn't people in operas get stabbed and poisoned? Didn't they die all over the stage? Then she wouldn't have to sing! *So, let it happen to me now!* Daisy prayed.

She cleared her throat and licked her lips.

* * *

...'Ah, me! Poor Daisy! Daisy, my love!'
A handsome man with a black moustache
and a long velvet cloak wept tunefully.

Daisy, stabbed through the heart,
gazed up at him. 'I die!' she whispered.

'Don't leave me!' Moustachio Man
sang in Italian. Six times.

'I die!' Daisy whispered again. No time
to sing her goodbyes. Just two quick
whispers and she was gone.

'Ah me!' Heartbroken Man covered her with his cloak. He went to the front of the stage and sang some more...

'Magnificent, Daisy! Well done, Leonie!' Miss Ambler clapped her hands.

Had she done it? Had she sung the whole song?

There was a pause, then the whole class cheered.

Yes, it was over. She must have sung *You-don't-love-me* from start to finish!

'That was so good we'll leave it in whether Nathan gets better or not!' the teacher decided. There was a smile on her face for the first time in weeks.

'Daisy, you're such a dark horse!' she teased. 'Just wait until I tell Mrs Waymann and Mrs Hunt – they'll never believe that you have a hidden talent!'

'Nice one!' Leonie grinned at Daisy as Bernie King came into the hall to interrupt Miss Ambler.

Daisy sat down with a bump. 'Was it OK?' she asked Jimmy.

He gave her a thumbs-up signal. 'Ace!'

Over to her right, Winona sulked.

'And I take it everything's under control for tonight?' King was asking Miss Ambler. 'You've handed out car-parking tickets and such like?'

'Erm–' Scatty Ambler obviously hadn't.

The caretaker sighed. 'You've arranged for chairs to be put out in the hall?'

'Er–'

Bernie sucked in air between his teeth. 'But you've made sure that all the private areas of the school will be kept securely locked – the storerooms, the IT room, the staff toilets etcetera?'

Miss Ambler looked faint at the tasks still ahead.

'Never mind, leave it all to me,' Bernie said smugly. Without him, Woodbridge Junior would fall apart at the seams. 'I'll put out the chairs and lock up, see that everything runs smoothly.'

Rambler Ambler thanked him over and over. 'Oh and Mr King,' she added. 'I can still rely on you to work the stage lights and the sound board during the performance, can't I?'

Caretaker-of-the-Year polished his halo. He nodded and winked. Bernie King actually winked. 'You bet you can rely on me, Louise,' he assured her.

Everyone giggled. *Louise!*

'Seven o'clock on the dot!' Bernie said. 'Don't worry, I'll be here!'

'Daisy!' A voice called.

She'd cut across the park on her way home from school, trying to drive the words of her stupid song out of her head. OK, so she'd proved she could sing. OK, so her mum and dad would be thrilled. But she still wished she could be stabbed and die a dramatic death instead. Like, it was mega embarrassing to sing about love and stuff.

'Daisy!' the voice called again.

She stopped by the duck pond and turned

to see Maya running after her.

'I've been trying to catch up with you all the way from Woodbridge Road!' she gasped. 'I want to tell you something.'

Quack-quack. The ducks gathered by the edge of the pond, hoping for scraps of bread.

'Make it quick,' Daisy told her dark-haired friend. 'I've gotta go home and get changed into clean uniform for this stupid concert!'

'It's about Legs,' Maya told her, still breathless.

Ouch! The spider's name hit a sore place in Daisy's memory. *Poor Legs, rest in peace.*

'I think I just saw him!' Maya whispered.

Not again! Legs was gone. He was no more. 'How come?' Daisy quizzed. 'Are you sure it was him?'

As Maya shook her head, her long pony-tail swished. 'Not absolutely sure,' she admitted. 'But I was coming out of school through the yard outside Bernie King's office and I saw Lennox jumping up and barking.'

'So, what's new?' Fat Lennox always barked.

Maya nodded. 'Yeah, I know. So I was walking on. Then I looked again to see what had made Lennox mad. I couldn't spot anything at first.'

Quack! The ducks grew angry. *Where's the bread?*

'So you took a closer look?' Daisy asked.

'Yeah. And guess what? He was jumping up to try and catch this big, hairy spider. But the spider kept letting himself down on a thread and bouncing back up again–'

'Stop!' Daisy yelled. 'That was Legs all right!'

Quack! Quack!

'But you said he was dead!' Maya reminded her.

'I said Waymann swooshed him down the plug-hole!' Daisy hissed back. 'I said I *thought* he was dead!'

'Oh Daisy!' Maya took a step back and gave her a serious look.

Quack! Bread, bread, bread!

'What d'you mean, "Oh Daisy!"?' she demanded. 'Legs went down the sink into the drain. Schluck! Gone!'

Maya blinked, hesitated, then spoke out. 'Didn't you know that spiders can swim?'

'Swim?' Daisy echoed.

'Yes. They curl into a ball and float. You can swish them out of the bath down the plug hole, go away and find that they crawl right back. You know what spiders are like!'

"Incy-wincy spider, climbing up the spout" ...Of course!

'So Legs got swooshed down the sink, swam a bit and probably came up through the drain outside Bernie's office,' Maya explained.

Not dead, then? No. Super-spider had white water rafted down the drain! He'd climbed out like Incy-wincy to annoy Fat Lennox.

Alive! Daisy breathed. *Legs lives to fight another day!*

Seven

'Hurry up!' Daisy begged her mum.

Angie was giving last minute instructions to the babysitter about what to do if Mia woke while they were out.

'Come on, Dad. Let's go and start the car!' Daisy couldn't wait any longer. At this rate, she'd have no time to look for Legs before the start of the concert.

She had it all worked out. She would arrive

at school at 6.30 pm. She would sneak off to
Bernie King's office and entice Legs out of
hiding with a dead fly she'd collected in an
empty jam-jar.

*...Jungle Jane Morelli crouched quietly
behind a giant palm tree. She pulled a
creeper to one side to spy on the trap
she'd just set.*

*Three metres should be deep enough
for the hole she'd dug. And the smell of
dead anteaters should tempt the enemy
nicely. Jane had sweated under the
midday sun, covering the pit with
brushwood and leaves so that the Beast
of Borongi wouldn't see it.*

*The Beast was close now. Jungle Jane
could hear him crashing through the
bushes, breathing heavily.*

*The sun beat down. She sweated.
Would the Beast fall for the trick? Or
would he catch the scent of Jane herself,
hiding nervously behind the tree?*

Hmm. Years of hunting jungle monsters told Morelli to climb high, out of reach of the Beast of Borongi's terrible claws. So she shinned up the straight trunk, clinging to creepers as she went. Then she waited.

And waited.

Until at last the Beast burst into the clearing where she'd dug her pit. He stood on his hind legs and beat his chest, teetering on the edge of her trap.

One more step! Jungle Jane prayed.

But the Beast had spotted her up in the tree. He was turning away from the trap.

So Jane grabbed the long creeper and launched herself through the air. She swung towards the Beast. 'Oooaaayaah!'

Thud! Morelli's feet thumped against the Beast's chest. The Beast staggered. His mean eyes rolled, he let out an angry roar, then plunged into the deep, deep pit...

'OK, I'm ready!' Angie was out of breath as she climbed into the car.

Daisy hoped she could still make time to trap Legs and return him to Nathan before the start of the concert. *Hurry, hurry!* She sat on the edge of the back seat, urging her dad to jump the lights.

Ten long minutes passed. They arrived at school at the same time as a dozen other cars all looking for spaces to park.

Hurry, hurry!

Miss Ambler appeared in the car park, running scattily here and there. She saw Daisy get out of the car.

'Daisy, go and help Leonie and Jimmy to set out chairs in the hall!'

'B-b-but!' She had more important things to do.

Miss Ambler shooed her inside. 'Jared, help Kyle bring out the instruments. Winona, you carry on searching!'

Daisy found herself hustled into the hall. 'What are you doing?' she muttered to Winona.

'I'm looking for Bernie King,' came the

prim reply.

'Rather you than me.' Daisy stumbled over Fat Lennox who had parked his squat body across the doorway into the hall. The dog looked almost as glum as Nathan, who hovered nearby.

'Hey, Nathan, good news!' Daisy began. But the sound of chairs being scraped across the floor drowned out her voice.

Maybe that was just as well, Daisy thought. Perhaps she'd better check out Maya's latest sighting before she raised Nathan's hopes.

But she only had fifteen minutes left before the start of the concert. And the whole hall was in chaos.

Leonie and Jimmy were dragging chairs into place as fast as they could. Parents queued to sit down. Little Year 2s wandered around looking for their yoghurt pots.

'Where's Mr King?' Ambler bleated as she ran back into the hall. She was all dressed up for the big night in a long black skirt and a sparkly top. 'Hasn't anybody seen him? Oh dear, whatever shall we do?'

Daisy ran up to Leonie. 'What's with Ambler?' she asked. After all, it was only Bernie who thought he ran the school single handed. Nobody else cared whether he was around or not.

'King's gone missing,' Leonie reported.

'I know.' Daisy looked round for an escape route. She had serious stuff like catching Legs to think about. 'So?'

Leonie stopped arranging chairs and stared at her. 'Wake up, Daisy. What's King supposed to be doing tonight?'

Organising the car park, setting out seats, locking doors... Daisy still didn't get what all the fuss was about.

Leonie filled her in at last. 'Bernie's working the lights and the sound. He's the only one who knows how. Without him, the show can't go on!'

For a split second Daisy grinned. *Yeah; no*

concert! No yoghurt pots. No stupid solo.

But then she thought again.

All the work, all the rehearsals. All the parents sitting down to watch, not knowing that Bernie King had gone missing.

Daisy fell into a deeper study of the problem.

'Give us a hand,' Jimmy told Daisy as he dragged a stack of chairs past her.

'Not now. I'm thinking,' she muttered.

Where had Bernie got to? Why had he left Lennox behind? The dog lolled unhappily at the door, eyes drooping, jaws sagging.

Maybe the caretaker had had an accident? Daisy frowned. She went over to Lennox. 'What happened? Did he fall off a ladder? Did he break something?'

Lennox looked up with a bloodshot eye.

'Or did he lock himself in a room by mistake?' she suggested.

The fat dog pricked up one floppy ear and struggled to his feet. He panted loudly.

Daisy stared. Was that a coincidence, or

what? Lennox had definitely heard her say the words "locked in" and perked up.

'He did, didn't he?' she gasped. 'He was going around with his keys, making the IT room and the storerooms secure…'

'Huh – uhuh – huh!' Lennox panted. He set off down the corridor towards Waymann's lair. Waddle – waddle.

'Come back. The IT room's this way!' Daisy protested.

Lennox ignored her. He padded on past Hannam's office, then stopped at the door beyond.

The staff loo! Daisy saw the whole thing in a blinding flash.

Bernie had included the cloakroom in his security check-list. He must have gone inside and somehow locked himself in by mistake. Now Lennox was leading her to him.

So she sprinted down the corridor until she came to the loo.

'Mr King?' she called through the closed door. A bunch of keys swung from the lock.

Huh-huh-uhuh! Lennox joined in with a loud wheeze.

There was a dull thud from inside the tiny room. And another.

Someone was thumping his fist on the door. 'Help!' a deep voice begged. 'Unlock the door and get me out of here!'

'Daisy Morelli saved the show!' Miss Ambler had explained the reason why the start of the concert had been delayed to the audience.

Bernie King had got over his ordeal and taken up his position behind the rows of switches that worked the sound and the lights. They were ready at last.

Seated beside Jimmy on the big drum, Daisy could see her mum and dad nodding proudly from the front row.

A sea of faces sat behind them, all smiling expectantly. Ambler had put up her hair with a smart silver clasp. She turned her back to the audience and tapped her stick.

Daisy and Year 2 led into the opening

number with their yoghurt pot drums.

Bee-bop-bop-bop. Boppa-bop.

…'That went well!' Leonie grinned at Daisy as everyone clapped.

Year 2 stood up and took a bow.

Then Winona *brrum-brrum-be-deedlied* through her keyboard piece.

…'Hmm,' Leonie sniffed as Winona sat down. 'Not bad.'

The audience clapped again and stamped their feet.

Leonie took up her guitar. Daisy got shakily to her feet.

Da-da da-da da-dum… Leonie strummed the opening bars.

Daisy opened her mouth and sang.

Like a bird. Like a song thrush. Like a nightingale. Her voice trilled over the notes. *'You-don't love me may-be, But ju-u-ust sup-posing I-I-I – love you!'*

'Brilliant!' 'Wonderful!' Everyone stood up and cheered.

Angie and Gianni were beaming at her

from the front row.

Their Daisy was the star of the show.

Daisy bowed and grinned back at her mum and dad. Then she sat down with a satisfied sigh. This singing stuff wasn't so bad after all.

'Now, Nathan…?' Miss Ambler turned to her sad, sick pupil. 'Will you play for me?' she whispered.

With shaky hands, Nathan took his violin out of its case. 'I'll try, Miss,' he murmured.

And the whole hall fell silent.

Slowly Nathan began his Strauss waltz. 1-2-3, 1-2-3; sad and quiet at first, sending a small chill down the spine.

Miss Ambler waved her stick and Nathan's violin grew louder.

He peered over the rim of his glasses at the notes on his sheet of music and swept his bow across the taut strings.

'Is Nathan brave, or what?' Daisy whispered to Jimmy.

1-2-3, 1-2-3. Nathan's waltz picked up speed.

Daisy saw his grey eyes light up behind
the round glasses. A flush of colour spread
across his cheeks.

1-2-3, 1-2-3, 1-2-3! The waltz took off.

What was Nathan looking at, Daisy
wondered. Not the notes any more. His gaze
had wandered from the sheet and he played
without reading the music.

No, he was staring at the back of Winona's
pure white, clean, crisp shirt.

Daisy took in Mizz Perfect's long, golden
curls and sparkling blouse. 1-2-3, 1-2-3. A
black, moving object turned in circles, as if
waltzing. The World's Only Waltzing Spider
lifted his legs and danced to Nathan's tune.

'Winona, don't move!' Daisy squeaked out
a warning.

Winona squirmed around and shot her a
cross look. 'Ssshhh!'

Legs clung on to Winona's shirt and
danced on.

'It's Legs! Can you grab him?' Nathan
muttered to Daisy as he sawed his bow

across the strings. 1-2-3.

Easier said than done. How did you grab a runaway spider crawling over someone's shirt in the middle of a concert? Especially when that someone was Win-(ugh-I-hate-spiders)-ona Jones!

But if Daisy didn't act fast, Legs could easily leg it all over again.

So she looked round for something that would help.

Yoghurt pot! It was under her chair; exactly the right size to trap a dancing spider.

Slowly, easing her hand to the floor, Daisy grasped the plastic pot.

Even more slowly she raised it into the air.

Winona sat in front of her, swaying to the music. She didn't suspect a thing.

Smoothly, silently, Daisy leaned forward. She edged the pot towards Legs. It was six centimetres away... two... one.

Bop! Daisy landed the yoghurt pot on Winona's back. *Bullseye!* Winona gasped but didn't move. Daisy grinned. With her other hand she seized a sheet of Nathan's music and slid it under the pot. Then she lifted it clear; pot, paper, spider and all.

The concert was a huge success.

Nathan was picked out as a violinist with a brilliant future.

Winona's skill on the keyboard was noted. But the loudest praise of all was for Daisy's song.

'I've never heard a voice like it in a girl her age!' Jimmy's dad told Gianni. 'It must be her

Italian blood.'

Daisy's dad smiled and smiled.

'Charlotte Church, eat you heart out!' Mrs
Flowers said to Angie. 'That girl of yours
could be worth a fortune!'

Daisy didn't hear any of this because she
was busy returning Legs to Nathan's jam-jar.

Nathan was speechless. His eyes shone
with tears of joy. His whole face and his
sticky-up hair came back to life as he
watched Daisy pop Legs into the jar.

Then Ambler came and gave her star singer a hug. She dragged Daisy across to speak with Mr and Mrs Morelli.

'Your daughter has real talent,' she gushed, while Daisy squirmed and blushed. 'You should be very proud.'

'*Si!*' Gianni nodded, his face split in two by a smile. 'We are!'

Then scatty Rambler Ambler went and remembered the very thing Daisy had assumed she would have forgotten.

Her face went suddenly serious. 'But how's your other poor little girl?' she asked anxiously.

Aaagh! Daisy screwed up her eyes and tried to back away.

'Mia?' Angie replied, giving Daisy a darkly suspicious look.

Aaagh! Vanish me! Make me disappear in a puff of smoke!

'She's fine,' her mum went on, frowning suspiciously at Daisy. 'Horribly healthy, in fact... Why do you ask...?'

Look out for other Definitely Daisy
adventures!

What's the Matter, Maya?

Jenny Oldfield

Shock, horror... Bernie King discovers deep
holes in the school soccer pitch! When the
angry caretaker accuses an innocent dog,
only shy Maya knows that he's covering up
for his own pet. But she's too scared to
tell on Fat Lennox. Can Daisy finger the
real culprit?